HOUSEWIFE

SHREYEE HALDER

Made with ♥ on the Notion Press Platform
www.notionpress.com

To all who read to live.

Contents

FOREWORD

All character in the story are purely fictional. Any resemblence to any person dead or alive is completely coincidental.

ACKNOWLEDGEMENTS

To life, Family and Friends.

Prologue

Life of a housewife. The one with most controversy, specially in an Indian society. A housewife is now a days called as homemakers. But did the society really change.... With this fancy name did the actual scenario change? How many are allowed to fulfill their dreams ? How many can do what they want ? How many are actually free???? So many questions....So many doubts...so little said...So much left unsaid.

Sobha is a housewife or rather in recent times a homemaker. Let's not use her title. Let's not tag her by her father's or husband's identity. Let's get to know Sobha... Her life....her struggle... Her desicion that gave her immense pain but reflects the truth of our "Indian society".

Through the open window the blue sky and green field seemed just at an arm's length. But the bars of the window always seemed to block the view. Early every morning Sobha loved to see the surroundings. The way people moved around in the joggers park...the chirping of the birds...the early morning vendors. She loved everything about this town. It's been 8 years she is living here. After her BA she got married to Abhas Chatterjee. Though she was never very careerist she always wanted to follow her passion in music. If not as a career option but atleast as an engagement. But life doesn't follow our plans. The approach of a 6 digit salary groom with high chances of settling abroad changed her life upside down. Everybody told Sobha "not everybody is as lucky as you are". And it's been 8 years Sobha has been thanking her luck since then. Today is her ninth wedding anniversary. She is eagerly waiting for her husband's phone call. He is in away in Germany with a very important office project. This is not the first time he is away on such an auspicious day. Abhas always said "special days will come and go every year but opportunities once gone never returns". So Sobha never told him anything. Her four years old daughter Maya comes out and runs into her arms. Sobha smiled. Maya was way to young to wish her. Suddenly Sobha realised she has been sitting idle for a long time. So much work is yet to be done... getting Maya ready for school, making her tiffin , dropping her at school, on the way back she has to also buy vegetables, wash the clothes, put them to day, prepare the lunch, clean the house. She cursed herself for sitting and wasting time.

It was around 2:15 Sobha was just leaving the house to pick Maya from school when the phone rang. She ran to receive it. With trembling hands she picked it up and placed it near her ears. "*Hello*". Sobha felt like the newly wed wife eagerly waiting for her husband on their first night. Her hands and feet were already sweating. She could hear her heart beat that was almost about to stop. The voice from the other end made her hear beat run.

"Sobha?"

"Yes"

"Happy wedding anniversary".

"Same to you Abhas" she smiled on her own." *I have your gift ready"*

"O good. How is Maya?"

"She is good. How are you?"

"I am good. My return has been delayed by few more weeks . After few minutes of awkward silence Abhas said," *Sobha I am very busy. I will ring you later. Take care. Bye"*

Sobha's anniversary celebration was over. But even Abhas was not to be blamed. He was a really caring husband and father. But he looked at things differently. Abhas had always been into books. He never thought too much about girlfriend, wife, marriage etc. When his friends were busy changing girlfriends he was busy with his studies. He always believed in earning more to get his family a comfortable life. And he was ready to sacrifice anything for it.

While returning from the market along with Maya, Sobha saw a huge rustle. Tempo was fully loaded. And the workers were sweating like pigs in the early November. A man was shifting in their society. He was busy giving instructions to the workers. He looked somewhat in his mid thirties. Sobha did not like the way he was dressed. Loose black t shirt, three quarter brown pants, unshaved beard, tattoo in his right arm, unorganized long hair. She held Maya's hand firmly and walked inside her house.

After completing her days work Sobha came out and stood in her balcony for some fresh air. She looked up at the sky and saw the twinkling stars and went down her memory lane. The day she had stepped in here as a bride. The day Maya was born, who is fast asleep now, the first time Maya spoke, the first time she walked. So many memories. She never felt not doing her job or not pursuing her passion in music made her miss anything in life. Suddenly she heard a very sweet flute tune. She loved it. She realised it was flowing from the new neighbour's house. After few minutes she couldn't resist more. She locked Maya safely and left the house. After two or three seconds of awkwardness she rang the doorbell. The man she saw in the morning opened the door. Sobha said in a meek voice" *sorry for disturbing you so late. Actually I heard a sweet flute tune and couldn't resist myself. I had just come to meet the instrumentalists."* The man smiled and asked her to enter. It was a simple house with one bedroom, one kitchen, one washroom, and a long drawing room. The walls of the drawing room was covered with posters of musicians, singers of various countries. In one corner of the room the synthesiser, guitar were waiting to be played. The man handed Sobha a glass of water and smiled. Sobha took the glass and said *"thanks for entertaining your intruder".* In turn he smiled and said" *if the intruder is so beautiful then I would like to be intruded again and again."* Sobha felt a bit uneasy. She thought she shouldn't have come here. The man smiled and said " *relax I am not harmful. My name is Abhimanyu. You can call me Abhi. And I am the owner of this house and a passionate musician. And am struggling to make ends meet . That's all about me."* The way Abhi moved his hands and legs and shaked his hair while giving his introduction Sobha laughed her heart out. Next Sobha introduced herself. She also mentioned her passion in music. So he asked her why she didn't continue her passion which pulled into the topic of marriage responsibility and stuff. So Abhi said that is why he will not get married. Almost after one hour Sobha realised it was getting late. Sobha laughed a lot after many years. Spending her life within the four walls had stuffed her in a box . Today, after a long time she unveiled herself. Her dreams, her wishes, her aspirations, her likes , her dislikes she shared with someone. After an hour she stood up to say bye when Abhi said *" Don't say bye..say see you soon." Sobha smiled and left.*

Sobha felt different. She felt like she had spoken to her own self. She did not know what to call Abhi but he was definitely much more than just a neighbour. With passing days Sobha found a great friend in Abhi. The long lost Sobha which had fallen asleep after her marriage was waken up by Abhi. Morning texts, waving at the window, late night chats became slowly common to them. Chats got promoted to phone calls and sometimes even video calls. Few words, little music, and Abhi's non stop nonsense made things really interesting for Sobha.

Days passed and the neighbour became a friend. Sobha's husband had still not returned. He was sent on another project to California. But this time Sobha didn't miss Abhas. For she had no time to do so. She was busy helping Abhi with his new composition. Abhi had finally got a producer for his first album. Sobha stayed up during nights and helped Abhi. Abhi's friends also appreciated Sobha's taste in music. Finally the red letter day arrived. It was Abhi's music launch. Sobha accompanied him to the seven star hotel where the launch would happen. Sobha got Maya ready and sent her downstairs along with Abhi's friends to wait. She took out the best Sare from her wardrobe. She had kept this Sare untouched to be worn on a special occasion.

Abhi entered the room and was stunned. He had never seen this lady in front of him before. Red Sare, organised long hair, bracelet and watch on her wrist, kajal, lipstick and that smile ...the best smile he could imagine. Sobha turned around and said" I am so sorry abhi I took so much time to get ready. Actually I couldn't understand what to wear. Actually I have never been to such an occasion before". As Sobha kept rattling Abhi walked towards her with slow steps and whispered in her ear " you look perfect." Sobha blushed. Abhi continued "only one thing is missing". Abhi took out a red box form his pocket and handed it to Sobha. She opened it to find a pair of earrings inside. Sobha turned towards the mirror and wore the earrings. She smiled at Abhi's reflection on the mirror and he smiled back. A loud horn from below was heard. Abhi and Sobha looked down to find their friends Sourav, Nikita, Pankaj, Vikas and Payal waiting for them with Maya in Sourav's arms.

After an hour's drive they reached the banquet. As soon as Abhi stepped in there was a huge rustle. The producer of their album Mr A Sen cordially welcomed them. There were many invites from the music world. Finally the press meet began. Everybody praised Abhi for his wonderful work. Finally Abhi rose to share some words. Sitting between the audiences Sobha felt Abhi was so far from her. She couldn't believe it the same person who has helped her when her daughter was suffering from fever at midnight and there was no to call for help, she couldn't realise this was the same person who picked Maya from school when she was sick, this was the same Abhi with whom she shared her pains and found a wonderful friend. She sat glaring at him. Abhi cleared his throat and began" there are so may things to say that I don't know where to begin and where to end". He thanked his parents friends his procedure music teacher his destiny. Finally he said " last and the most important names without whom nothing would have been possible. My inspiration and the lady behind my success Sobha" he pointed towards her as the entire crowd turned towards her. " and her beautiful daughter maya". Mr Sen request Sobha to join Abhi on the stage to unveil their music album poster. She held maya's hand firmly and walked forward. Together they drew the curtains before the poster. The title read as: ***Music The universal language of Love.***

Sobha was a bit perplexed. She walked up to Abhi and said" Abhi there is a mistake in the cover. My surname is not printed." Abhi smiled and said" there is no mistake. It is not printed because there is no need of it. The credit is for you. And the surname is not yours. So it is not printed." Sobha felt a gush of emotions within her. Abhi handed her a copy of the album and whispered into her ears" thank you". A tear escaped Sobha's eyes.

Sobha tried to contact Abhas to share her great achievement but couldn't. She shared this news with her parents whose first reaction was" does Abhas know you are getting friendly with a stranger?" Sobha sighed and said no. They seemed extremely worried. She told them that due to some problem she was not able to connect with him in Germany. Even her in laws did not accept this news happily. All the promises " you can continue your studies after your marriage. You can follow your passion even after you become a mother" started to show how hollow it was. But she believed that Abhas would support her. She eagerly waited to share the news with him. In the meantime there was a success party thrown my Mr Sen for the great success of their album. Since the party would continue till late at night Abhi had suggested to leave Maya in the house with her maid. The party was a memorable moment in Sobha's life. She had never imagined that she would be able to see the singing stars from so close. Talking to them, clicking photos, shaking hands, Sobha lost track of time. She returned home only to find Abhas waiting for her. The fire blazing in Abhas's eyes said everything. Sobha had no guts to tell him about her new achievement.

Abhas slammed the door, turned to Sobha, handed her a few newspaper cuttings and magazines. In bold and black it was written" ***Who is SOBHA? What is the truth that the recently famous singer Abhimanyu hiding? Or is there something he is not disclosing?"*** . Sobha was moved to tears. She was so overwhelmed with the success story that she had ignored the paparazzi. She looked at Abhas who questioned her" I hope you have a satisfying explanation to these. And since when have you been so much irresponsible to leave Maya with maid pray I know?". "Abhi had asked me to do so". She had placed the exact wrong words at the exact wrong time. Abhas raised his voice and said " I have no words to say. I hope you can realise the amount of mess you have created. You are old enough to realise what you need to do. Such things will not be tolerated again and again. You know the amount of humiliation my parents had to face. From the day of our marriage they kept on saying leave Sobha and Maya with us. But I argued with them and allowed you to stay on your own. For I didn't want anyone to interfere in your life. I allowed you all your freedom. But if this is how you use it then I have to take a decision. This can't continue. Mom is really sick with all these rubbish. I am leaving to meet her. Next morning when I return I need to see all these mess cleared." He pointed to the music lyrics she had written. Sobha nodded as the most dutiful wife. Abhas left. But his presence did not. Sobha could feel his words reverberating around her. She could almost imagine the pain her family had felt because of her selfishness. Tears rolled down her eyes. She decided to stop everything and return to her normal life. She rang Abhi but strangely couldn't speak. She kept crying over the phone and disconnected it. Abhi ran to her house only to find Sobha on the floor crying like hell. He gave her a glass of water and sat beside her. She narrated the entire incident. She said she never wanted to meet him again and handed over all her work to him and asked him to leave. Abhi left without speaking a single word.

The cold atmosphere in Sobha's house prevailed. Abhas was off for another project. But this time his mother came to stay along with Sobha. Sobha was kept in house arrest. Sobha had shut the window facing Abhi's house. She couldn't bear looking at the celeb page of the newspaper which was covered with the news of the new rising star **"ABHIMANYU"**. Strangely Sobha found the more she tried to disconnect herself with music the more connected she felt. She couldn't resist the temptations to meet Abhi when his music flowed to her room. The more she tried to cover her ears the clearer the music became. Unable to bear this she rang Abhi one afternoon when Maya was at school and her mother-in-law was sleeping. For one complete hour none of them spoke. Sobha kept crying, sobbing and sniffing. Though there were no exchange of words Sobha felt so light and relaxed. She didn't understand what actually was happening to her and want she actually wanted. After a week the phone rang with a sad news. Abhas's father was not well and Sobha's mother-in-law had to leave unwillingly. Abhas had consoled her that Sobha would not repeat it. Sobha had also promised Abhas that she would behave as she was expected. One afternoon the door bell rang. Sobha opened the door and stood still. Abhi entered on his own and latched the door. The self controlled Sobha lost herself in his arms and stared crying insistently. Abhi soothed her. He told her that there is a party in his house for he has received the best debut singer of the year and he wants her to join him. " I can't think of celebrating my success without my inspiration". Sobha couldn't resist. She promised to be there.

On the selected day she had sent Maya to her grandparents house. She got ready and left. On reaching Abhi's house she could feel the change. It was no more the unkept unorganized house of a struggling bachelor. It looked contended just as Abhi's present situation. She could feel the touch of music in her as well as his life. She was warmly welcomed by Sourav and payal. She meet the other friends as well. She met the remaining guests. And finally stood before Abhi. She almost didn't recognise him. The young gentleman in black suit looked so charming. She just couldn't remove her eyes from him just as few months back he couldn't when they were leaving for the album release. Abhi turned but didn't see Sobha rather he watched her eyes...those eyes that kept glowing even in the darkness of his life. That smile which kept him going. That said" everything is going to be fine" . And.... And those earrings. The day couldn't have been better for Abhi.

The party went well. Everybody present was busy congratulating Abhi for his success. But neither Sobha nor Abhi spoke to each other. Sourav said in despair "so sad. The two who never stopped chatting with one another have become the definition of distance." Payal said" the world is still not easy for girls. Specially with married girls". Everybody was silent but all agreed. The society that we live ...the society that should pave the smooth road for the next generation...that should uphold culture....has become the biggest enemy to lives of happy people. Suddenly Mr Sen drew everybody's eyes towards the stage. He cleared his throat and said "our dear friend Abhi has something to say... A message to give... A small glimpse of what our next album would contain". The press became very active with an instant. Abhi took the stage, held the mic lowered his head and said"***Tonight don't insist on leaving. Just sit like this close to my soul. Don't say words like I will die or I will be lost. If anything happens to you I won't be alive. Just ponder for a while why shouldn't I stop you? My soul seems to be leaving....cause you are my soul.***

Keep this request of mine please. Tonight don't insist on leaving." Everybody clapped but no one got the words except Sobha. These were the lyrics she had been translating for him form a song and has given him that day when they met last. Completion his speech Abhi looked straight towards Sobha. He could read from her face she got what he was trying to convey.

The party ended. She hugged Payal and Nikita and shook hands with Sourav Pankaj and Vikas as they left. Abhi waved to them at the door and turned around just when Sobha stepped to leave. He latched the main door. Sobha got confused. Abhi never behaved in this manner. But she smiled. Cause this was the Abhi she knew. Always mischievous with his small little surprises. Abhi said "I am not letting you go without the translation.". Sobha knew well what Abhi indicated at. Still she said "I didn't get you". Abhi smiled and said "you got me since the day we have met". Sobha couldn't smile as earlier. Sobha was used to Abhi's tone. He never meant anything bad. He spoke in this same manner to every girl. But today there was something different. Something that Sobha saw for the first time. Still she smiled as always ignoring the fact. Abhi said "translation please". And Sobha sang like the nightingale **"Aj Jane ki zid na Karo....."** With each line Abhi took a step closer to her. And finally when Sobha said**"Aj Jane ki zid na Karo"** Abhi slipped his arms around her and immediately Sobha lost herself within his arms and said" I can't explain how I missed everything. It was so difficult for me." He whispered " I know". He released her and took her face in his hands and said "I love you". For a moment

Sobha forgot she had a world outside. They had two different worlds. Nothing seemed important to her. It all seemed to flow like music. They came so close they could actually feel each others breath. Sobha closed her eyes. She felt she had achieved what she was supposed to. But suddenly she realised that this fantasy was not something she should brew. She had promises to keep. She felt as if this moment was not something that was supposed to happen. She held lose Abhi in a jerk and rushed towards the door. But she turned to see Abhi who stood startled and smiled towards him. Abhi had seen what he wanted . He got his answer. Sobha rushed back home. She turned the key only to find it the door was open. She entered and saw her husband and mother-in-law waiting for her. Her hands and feet which were already sweating stared to perspire. Abhas said in a low but grave voice " where have you been?" Somehow Sobha mustered all her strength and said" I .... I went to Abhi's house to attend the party". Now Abhas raised his voice " o I see. So this was all pre planned. Do you even know the number to times I have rang you? We all were so worried that we were forced to call the neighbour who told us you went to Abhi's house". Sobha stood straight and thought she has to say if not now then never. She has to make them understand. She said in a low and submissive voice " Abhas you are getting it all wrong. Abhi was a very good friend. He helped me to spend my time fruitfully when I had nothing to do". Abhas raised his eyebrows and said" he has moulded you well I can see". Abhas's mother now screamed " there is no point in wasting time with her. She doesn't care for us or our reputation. The way people around are gossiping about us it's so shameful. It's all because of her. Since afternoon Maya is crying for her mother". Suddenly Sobha became worried and looked towards Abhas. "She is sleeping in her room", Abhas said. " Sobha she is only four. She needs her mother. Do you even realise your responsibilities as a mother? What kind of a mother are you?". Unable to bear the question mark on her motherhood she replied sharply " what have I done that everyone of you are accusing me may I know? And it was you all who promised me to that I can follow my dreams. And when I am doing so why am I facing so many questions?" Abhas marked every word she said and signed. "It seems you have well settle yourself. And I don't find any need of myself. So I have taken a desicion that will be beneficial for both of us". Sobha shook sightly. Abhas continued " I have already spoken to the lawyer. He will get the divorce proceedings ready". Sobha's world crumpled within a moment. She started crying and begged " no Abhas don't do this. Think about our daughter. Please don't do this". " this is something I am doing for her good. Did you think what not she will have to face because of you. People will say her parents got divorced because her mother had an affair." They left leaving Sobha crying helplessly on the floor. The words kept ringing in her ears. Affair..... affair.... affair... No it was not an affair. But the entire world saw it in that manner. Or maybe it was. That moment between them? The confession of Abhi Was it an affair? What do affair mean? Being friendly to another man after marriage? What have I done to myself. Destroyed everything. Sobha started crying. She didn't get the courage to enter Maya's room. She felt extremely guilty. Suddenly the door cracked and

Abhi entered. “Why did you leave the main door open?” He was expecting answer when he saw Sobha on the floor. He sat beside her. With sobbing tone Sobha explained what had happened. Taking both her hands within his hands he looked straight into her eyes and said “lets leave Sobha”. Sobha was astonished. Abhi continued “ Sobha don’t think what people will say. You can’t force them to see from your shoes. Even if you sacrifice all your happiness they will speak shit. And nothing is left here that is yours. Pack all your things. Take Maya and leave with me”. Slowly she said “ but what if Abhas gets to know I am leaving with Maya ?” Abhi said “ I’ll take care of everything”. These words seemed more convincing to her than the vows Abhas had made during their marriage. Sobha had so much to say. But her lips only made a faint movement and no words were uttered. The sparkle in her moist eyes said everything and a similar sparkle was seen in Abhi’s eyes.

Sobha had packed everything. It was just the crack of dawn. The weak ray of sunlight entered through the open window and rested on her daughter who was sound asleep. Sobha picked up a newspaper and saw the news of suicide of a struggling musician. She turned the pages and read the other news when she heard the door bell ring. She ran to the door and stood startled. It was Abhas. “ I know you expected someone else. But just ponder for a while how many musicians reach Bombay everyday and how many are actually successful. Think about Maya. Will you be able to give her the life she deserves ? I am still ready to forget everything and begin new. Think about it and let me know. You are a responsible mother. I know that." Saying this Abhas left. Sobha was in great despair. She couldn't come to a conclusion. Abhas had handed her the tickets to where he had planned to take his family. Every word Abhas said was true. Abhi was still not successful. No one knows how long it will take. Will he ever be successful was also a dominant question. Sobha couldn't risk Maya's future. She swallowed her decision when her phone rang. Abhi from the other side seemed very excited " Sobha you won't believe what happened. I just rang the travel agent to speak about the tickets and he told me three tickets are available in today's morning flight. Pack everything and come straight to the airport. I will be waiting for you. You are so lucky for me Sobha ." With a grim voice Sobha said " Abhi I can't do this. I can't risk Maya's future. Abhas is ready to accept me. I will leave with him and my in laws. I am sorry Abhi but I....I have to do this" the last words jumbled as Sobha started crying. She didn't know what she did was correct or wrong. But this was the best she could have done for her daughter. She looked at the rising sun and wondered how a setting sun looked...

Sobha is just symbolic to the numerous women in society who had dreams in their eyes but never got an opportunity. Who was the villain to these lives? Who is the villain to our story? Abhas? Sobha's in laws? The society ? Or was it Sobha herself?

Printed by Libri Plureos GmbH in Hamburg,
Germany